安息日

守武はるみ

若い頃に作りためておいた俳句・英文俳句たちを、今回まとめて句集に致しました。タイトルの「安息日」は、カトリック・クリスチャンの洗礼を受けた私が、神が天地創造を終え、第七日目に安息をされたという、その「安息の日」という言葉から、ほのぼのとした気持ちを表した一句「安息の日なりひねもす着ぶくれて」を代表句としてつけました。

ひとりよがりの句集かとは思いますが、読者の皆様に何か感じとっていただけたら幸いと思います。また、歳を重ねた今、自分自身を表す一つの作品として出版の機会を得たことを嬉しく思います。

安 息 日

平成元年秋～平成四年

目次

鎮魂歌 ……………………………………… 3

梅雨晴 ……………………………………… 16

里の歌 ……………………………………… 29

安息日 ……………………………………… 42

讃岐路 ……………………………………… 55

鎮魂歌

春装の友と向き合ふティールーム

お喋りも満開となり花の昼

まだ里に父居るごとく弥生かな

Feeling as if

Father were still there in home

already March though

泣きそふな空に二月の鴉舞ふ

ひとことも残さず二月父逝けり

春浅く死すべきとして父逝けり

We're mortal

Father taught me at last

this spring by his death

春宵や父の戒名眺めをり

夭折を夢見てみたり春立つ夜

春蘭の己が匂ひに酔ふごとし

An orchid flower

intoxicated with its own fragrance

in spring air

犬山祭り三句

山車を組む声飛び交わせ花の昼

からくりの山車黒光り花の雨

花の雨肩車の子山車を追う

A boy piggyback

following a float

the rainy cherry blossoms

春の風邪寡黙の人となりており

愛犬も小さく欠伸下萌ゆる

春昼の立ち居物憂き美容室

A spring afternoon

feeling languid in movements

at a beauty shop

ふわふわと病み上がりの身山笑ふ

しばらくは枝垂桜の銀宇宙

釣り人は春昼の糸たらし居り

Hanging a line

an angler monopolizes

the spring afternoon

平成三年二月イラク停戦

淡雪の溶けて戦争終結す

双雛飾りて眉のゆるびけり

包むとき言葉かけやり雛仕舞ふ

One by one

playing with each

my girls stow away Hina dolls

漣の細かきことも瀬戸の春

鳥雲に入る法要に向ふ旅

忘却は人の幸なり春の雲

Oblivion—

human bliss

spring clouds

露の臺御膳に父の一周忌

春霖や御国の父へレクイエム

父偲ぶ時過ぎゆきて緑立つ

Time has passed

remembering dead Father

green leaves came out

平成四年長女美和小学校卒業

師の目にも光るものあり卒業す

紙風船明日のために又畳み

静止画に一艘流れ花の昼

A still picture

with cherry blossoms

a boat suddenly came into

格子戸に春日遊ばす旧家かな

春塵や御堂に灰と芭蕉像

俯かず揺れて雨受くチューリップ

Receiving rain

just swinging not drooping

—tulips

子犬抱く子の膝頭聖母祭

生受けて今日を四十路の復活祭

春深し濃ひ珈琲を淹れてをり

Somewhat monotonous

making a cup of strong coffee

in deep spring

梅　雨　晴

緋牡丹の首かしげをり雨後の昼

安曇野のグラスを透かす五月晴

ゆり椅子に居て五月雨の足速し

In a rocking chair

hearing the quick beat

early summer rain

若葉して昔日息吹く尼僧寺

田楽に集ふ人垣河畔茶屋

水溜まりドレミの音に走り梅雨

Do, Re, Mi,

a little pond sings

it's a rainy season

初夏の景細むまなこに入りきらず

黒百合や人恋ひし頃遠くして

母の日やお茶入れたよと末娘

"Tea is ready!"

younger daughter wakes me up

on Mother's Day

梅雨じめり新刷辞書の匂ひかな

容赦なく雨打ち続く桜桃忌

移り気を見て見ぬふりす四葩かな

Hydrangeas

pretending not to see me

my caprice

一片の迷ひ断つ朝髪洗ふ

冷蔵庫小さき平和の音たてる

梅雨しとどポスター展へ傘の花

Umbrella flowers

toward the poster gallery

in the middle of rainy season

身のうちの晴れてひと品胡瓜もむ

冷房の部屋真四角に窓堅し

洗濯機高く唸れり梅雨晴間

A fine day

washing machine keeps roaring

in the rainy season

草むしりつつ下校子の夏帽子

冷素麺網戸を渡る風軽し

よく響く木槌金槌梅雨晴間

Hammers and mallets

resounding in the sky

a lull in the rain

パステルの焼菓子並ぶパリ祭

大雪渓背にすシャガール美術館

雨粒の遊べる葉うら梅雨晴間

Raindrops

playing rolling on leaves

a lull in the rain

聖堂に入る胸ポケットにサングラス

聖堂に入りて涼しき昼下がり

香水の一滴ふひに淑女なる

A drop of perfume

all of the sudden

here's a lady

髷付けの力士ホームに朝涼し

冷奴食ぶも無口の父なりき

器にも気配りみえて夏料理

Summer dishes

appetizing

in cool-looking plates

緑蔭やみくじ吉とて安堵せり

夕涼にエプロン付ける厨かな

珈琲を挽く気になりぬ夜の秋

At night

a hint of autumn

makes me grind coffee beans

湯上がりに故郷の老舗の団扇かな

夏痩せのまなこ大きく古書開く

赤子泣く声静まりて夏の果て

Day by day

crying baby comes to calm down

end of the summer

里 の 歌

秋立ちて机上にペンの戻りけり

小鳥来る朝餉の卓の白布巾

ままごとの延々続く野分晴

The clear sky after a typhoon

children playing house

it seems endless

渋滞の旅より帰る終戦日

慣れし橋取り壊す音秋暑し

新しきアスファルト道秋暑し

Around my house

lingering summer heat

new asphalt roads

新蕎麦や自慢話に相槌し

母ありて厨の隅の新豆腐

潮風に秋蝉の声故郷なり

Sea breeze carrying

an autumn chorus of cicadae

my home town

栗ごはんふと口をつく里の歌

観音道香流れ来る秋日和

天守にて欄干秋の日を溜めぬ

At a donjon

warmth of the autumn sun

n the railings

円らにてたわわに撓ふ雨の萩

秒針の細かく秋の夕刻む

所在なく机に向かふ無月かな

Without the harvest moon

boredom makes me

sit at the desk

蜩や読経と競う寺の坂

母の背に続き来慣れし墓参道

菊抱く墓前の母の背は丸し

Before Father's tomb

holding chrysanthemums in her arms

mother's round back

爽やかに華燭の白きベールかな

コスモスの大輪風の信濃かな

冷やかに午前六時の雨戸繰る

Dry and cold sound

at six in the morning

opening the storm shutters

健やかな四肢踊らせて秋祭

十月やインクの匂ふ俳誌来る

ままごとの筵の子の目秋夕焼

Children's shining eyes

playing house on the straw mat

in the autumn sunset

待宵や母と久しく語り居し

温泉の白き湯に入る良夜かな

虫の音につひまどろみし終ひ風呂

In the bathtub

dozing with singing insects out

late at night

杓に酌む延命水とや秋の里

秋晴や瀬戸物市の千のこゑ

白釉へ秋日が撥ねる陶器市

Pottery glazed in white

reflecting autumn sunlight

at the street market

外国人増えて夜業の町工場

気の置けぬ話紅葉の昼餉かな

紅葉冷え新装なりし美術館

Among autumn leaves

its chilly first floor

newly-built museum

安らかな寝顔見飽きぬ夜長かな

縫針の呟きほどに秋思かな

カーラジオショパン流るる暮の秋

Driving the car

with Chopin's Nocturne on the radio

in the late autumn

安息日

踏みしめる砂利音雨の一葉忌

十一月風に揺らるる暦かな

子犬抱くかひなに伝ふ今朝の冬

Hugging a puppy

feeling winter has come

with her warmth

病み上がり山茶花の白眩しかり

ブティックの小物の色の小春かな

襟巻し朝幸福度少し増す

With a wool scarf

a little happier

than yesterday

短日や置かれしままの文庫本

悴かみし四肢のほころぶ湯槽かな

冬薔薇祈る形に天を指す

A winter rose

as if it were praying

directs to the sky

小春日や慣れた手つきの水仕事

銘々の好みの菜のおでんかな

かき卵ふわりと上がる冬の朝

Scrambled eggs done

soft and fluffy

a fine winter morning

冬日射す田畑煙れる瀬戸路かな

熱燗は野暮と言ひたる祖父なりき

父瘦すと聞き足鈍る冬帰省

Hesitating to go home

after hearing Father's getting thin

the winter holidays

裸木に星の掛かりて人を待つ

妬心ふと荒瀬に遊ぶ鴛鴦の群れ

皸の手に帯巻きて外出す

With a Band-Aid

on my chapped finger

going out into the winter town

寄鍋や買物籠に菜満てり

霜に堪へ松の子ちまと並びをり

安息の日なりひねもす着ぶくれて

Bundled up

all day long

the Sabbath

クリスマスキャンドルを買ふ小さき店

降誕祭人の間にふと心空く

遠き地の飢ゑし子等にも聖夜来ぬ

Christmas Eve's here

and also there – the farther place

on those starving children

幸分かつやうに切りゆく聖菓かな

聖樹飾る子等の瞳に光満つ

プレゼント解く目きらめくクリスマス

Unfold a present

sparkling eyes

on Christmas Day

マニキュアを粧ひて春待ちてをり

搗きたての餅の匂ひや白エプロン

賀状書く年経る毎の厚みかな

The older I get

the more New Year's cards

I write

大寒の波立てて入る湯槽かな

彼の寒さ巡りて父の三回忌

放浪者見る見られてる冬の街

Staring at a homeless

or staring back at me

on a cold street

春隣新幹線の窓透けて

春近しシャガール展に人集ふ

浮寝鳥憂きこと知らぬ首傾ぐ

As if worrying something

with her neck turned back

just sleepy water bird

讃 岐 路

方寸の庭にも満つる淑気かな

仁和寺の仁王和らぐ今朝の春

同じとも思へず今朝は年新た

Nothing's changed though

I can't help feeling something new

on this New Year's Day

一六タルト松過ぎに着く里便り

女正月湯の香の残る髪を梳く

瀬戸跨ぐ橋上列車初景色

A New Year's scenery

from the train on the bridge

crossing over the Inland sea

つづら折白き雨打つ淑気かな

初読や風の音聞く長寝椅子

讃岐路や円やかに落つ初入日

The sunset on New Year's Day

melting into the field of 'Sanuki'

mellowly

守武はるみ

１９５２年　香川県観音寺市生まれ
１９７０年　観音寺第一高等学校卒
１９７４年　同志社大学文学部英文科卒
１９８１年～１９８５年　米国・ニューヨーク市滞在
帰国後、名古屋市・犬山市の中日文化センター、NHK文化センター等で英会話講師を十年余務め、Jリーグ・名古屋グランパスの月刊サポーター誌のサッカー英語解説コラムも執筆した。
現在、愛知県丹羽郡大口町在住

安息日

2011年4月20日　初版発行

著　者　守　武　は　る　み

発行者　守　武　義　典

発行所　株式会社　虹有社（こうゆうしゃ）
東京都文京区小石川 1-1-12-1F
TEL 03-5684-1007　FAX03-5684-1008
http//www.kohyusha.co.jp
info@kohyusha.co.jp

・印刷　モリモト印刷株式会社
落丁・乱丁本はお取替え致します。
©Harumi Moritake 2011, Printed in Japan
ISBN 978-4-7709-0056-2　C 0092
定価は表紙に印刷してあります。